The Cloud Lasso

story by Stephanie Ellis Schlaifer
illustrated by Melodie Stacey

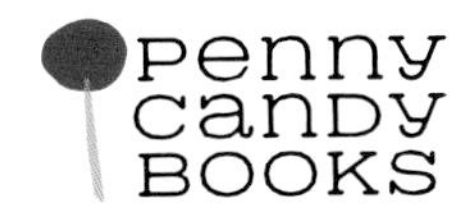

Penny Candy Books
Oklahoma City & Greensboro

This book is printed on paper certified to the environmental and social standards of the Forest Stewardship Council™ (FSC®).

Photo of Stephanie Ellis Schlaifer: Arny Nadler
Photo of Melodie Stacey: Richard Stacey
Design & lettering: Shanna Compton

23 22 21 20 19 1 2 3 4 5
ISBN-13: 978-0-9996584-4-4 (hardcover)

Small press. Big conversations.
www.pennycandybooks.com

For Jana —S. E. S

For my two grandpas, Ted and John —M. S.

Delilah could see nothing
but clouds for miles.

There'd been nothing
but clouds for days.

Nothing but nothing
since Doo-Dad had died.

Clouds covered the barn.

Clouds slumped over Delilah's head.
Even her pigtails drooped.

When her dogs, Oboe and Ibid, sneezed,
little clouds burst out of their noses.

Whenever things were gloomy, Doo-Dad had cheered Delilah up by teaching her how to do something new.

They built a chicken coop. And carved spoons.

They made ice cream after they milked the cows.

Delilah's grandpa was always doing something.
That's why she called him Doo-Dad.

Now it was too cloudy to do anything.
Delilah had had enough.

"*ENOUGH!*" she shouted.

Just then, a blue jay landed
on Delilah's head.

"Hey, that's Doo-Dad's!"

It was her grandpa's lasso.

Doo-Dad had been a champion at the rodeo.
Delilah couldn't even rope a sawhorse.

"C'mon," she grumbled to herself, impatiently.

She practiced on the fence post, like Doo-Dad had taught her.

But she missed.

And she missed.

And she missed *again*.

The day was getting even gloomier. Delilah huffed and flung the lasso over her head toward the sky.

But this time . . .
she caught something.

Delilah caught a *cloud*.

It looked a little like a turnip, and Delilah *hated* turnips. So did Doo-Dad.

She pulled it to the ground, and Oboe and Ibid barked and yelped . . .

and the cloud disappeared.

Blue sky peeked through where the cloud had been. It wasn't much, but it made a difference.

She tried again.

This time, Delilah roped a bigger cloud. It took some effort to get it down.

The dogs jumped all over it, and more blue sky appeared!

"Doo-Dad wouldn't believe *this*."

Again, Delilah hurled the lasso
toward the sky. This time,
she snagged a black cloud
as angry as a bull.

It sparked with lightning and howled with thunder.

The horses reared up at it, and Delilah held on tight to the rope until the cloud was gone.

Now, a ray of sunshine poked through.

Delilah twirled and swirled and hurled the lasso.

She roped a cloud shaped like a hairy spider.

And a cloud that looked like
Marcus, who teased her for
wearing overalls to school.

And one shaped like her chicken,
Mrs. Winner, who pecked
at her ankles.

(Doo-Dad never liked feeding
the chickens, either.)

And when a cloud floated
by shaped like the awful
dress she had to wear
for picture day, Delilah
yanked it down and
stomped on it *herself*.

Soon, there was nothing but blue sky all around her.

But she still didn't feel right.

Delilah looked down and saw a little cloud hanging right there over her heart.

It would not come off.

So, when a rainbow
appeared, Delilah swung
the lasso around it.

She pulled herself
up,
up,
up,
into the blue—
and the dogs, too.

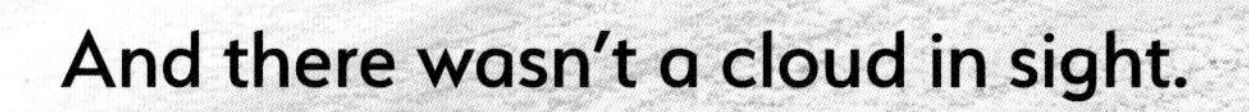

And there wasn't a cloud in sight.

Stephanie Ellis Schlaifer is a poet and installation artist in St. Louis. She is the author of *Cleavemark* (BOAAT Press, 2016) and has an MFA in poetry from the Iowa Writers' Workshop. Her poems and art have appeared in *Best New Poets*, *Georgia Review*, *Harvard Review*, *AGNI*, the *Offing*, *Denver Quarterly*, *LIT*, *Colorado Review*, *Fence*, on *PoetryNow*, a podcast of the Poetry Foundation, and elsewhere. She frequently collaborates with other artists, most recently with Cheryl Wassenaar on the installation "The Cabinet of Ordinary Affairs" at the Des Lee Gallery. *The Cloud Lasso* is her first children's book. Her work can be viewed at criticalbonnet.com.

Melodie Stacey is an artist and illustrator from Brighton, East Sussex, in the UK. She has exhibited her work in the UK and US and has worked with magazines such as *Flow* and *Pompom Quarterly* as an illustrator. *The Cloud Lasso* is her first picture book.